Janne Teller

WAR

What if it were here?

D1375358

Janne Teller

WAR

What if it were here?

Illustrated by Helle Vibeke Jensen

SIMON &
SCHUSTER

London · New York · Sydney · Toronto · New Delhi

A CBS COMPANY

What if Great Britain were at war.
Where would you go?

If the bombs had torn most of London, most of Britain,
to ruins? If the house that you and your family live in
had holes in the walls, all the windows broken, the roof
rent off? Winter is nearing, the heating doesn't work,
and the rain gushes straight in. You can only stay in the
basement. Your mother has bronchitis and yet another
bout of pneumonia on its way. Your older brother has
lost three fingers on his left hand in an episode with
a mine. He supports the Militia against the wishes
of your parents. Your little sister has been wounded
by grenade splinters and lies in a hospital with no
equipment. Your grandparents died when a bomb
struck their nursing home.

You yourself are still well and sound, but scared. Morning, midday, evening, night. You shudder every time the missiles whirl off far away, every time you see a glimmer of light on the horizon, not knowing if this time the missile is headed for you. You shudder every time the explosions sound. How many of your friends were struck this time?

The water pipes were blown up long ago. Every day you and your brother have to walk with two buckets each, through the streets and across Trafalgar Square to the public water truck. You have to run very fast across the square. Snipers hide in some of the buildings. Danes and Norwegians who have lived in Britain long enough to be mistaken for Britons. Not long enough to feel like one of us when war rages and the definition of friend and fiend resides in nationhood.

Worse than the fear is the hunger. Worst of all is the cold. You're cold all the time. And it's still only early November. You don't know how you're going to get through the winter. The doctor says that your mother won't survive another winter in the cellar. He can't help you find a better place, though. There are too many others who won't make it through another cold season in a cellar.

Your best friend has disappeared. His father was a Member of Parliament. In the new world, parliamentarians have no place. *Democracy led to the European Union and the European Union has broken down.* That's what they say. In the new world no one is allowed to call for democracy.

The father succeeded in getting out of the country. The family was supposed to follow. They didn't. Three days after the father left, the new Britification Police came for your friend and his little brother. The little brother showed up eight days later with one eye missing and strange movements of the head. He sits in a corner and nods all the time and says, I know nothing, I know nothing. The mother walks around the street, begging for food, asking for her eldest son even though rumours have it that he is dead. She can't leave as long as one son is missing. She can't leave no matter what: the country that has welcomed her husband doesn't believe in family reunification. She isn't personally persecuted, she can't get asylum.

You have stopped asking your father *where. Whereto* your family shall flee?

There is no answer to *where*. Your family has become a number. Five! No country wants another five refugees. Refugees who don't know the language, who don't know how to comport themselves in a classic cultural civilization, how to respect thy neighbour, place the guest before oneself, or how to protect the virtues of a woman. Refugees who don't know how to live in

the heat. No country wants to receive more of those decadent people from Great Britain. Free thinkers who are good for nothing but the corruption of the lives of the right-minded. They are unsuited for work. They don't speak Arabic, and they aren't used to carrying their load. Refugees from Britain are unable to do anything except sit in an office and turn over documents. Who needs that? That's what they say in the Arab world. The only region with peace and opportunities for a tomorrow. But where then?

Right before New Year's, against all odds, your father succeeds in getting in touch with some men arranging escapes. It is perilous and costs a lot of money, but your father has decided that it's necessary to save the family. Your mother is growing mad from the constant fear.

You have to sell whatever little you have left. It doesn't raise much money. No one has any means to pay. There's just enough to cover the travel and the false documents. The party membership cards are the most expensive. It's those that shall assert that you and your father have been politically active. It's those which may grant you access to asylum. Once you're safe, you'll all have to do your part to make a living. You're ready to do whatever. To sweep the streets or clean toilets. All you can think of is getting away from the bombs and the fear and the hunger and the freezing cold. Also your other grandmother has died. Your mother still has a chance of making it.

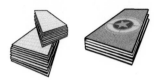

You could walk south to Folkestone and from there try to get across the tunnel to France. But there too, everything has broken down. No one in Europe has anything, there are no jobs, and there are already millions of refugees in miserable camps with hardly any food and no access to schools, health care or work. Your father wants to offer his family a future. He believes that the war will keep on for years. But one day you'll return home. That's why you must have an education, something to make a living off of when you go back.

You bet everything on this one chance. You have no idea if you shall ever see your uncles and aunts, your friends or your home again. You grit your teeth and try not to think about it. When at midnight you hurry from the lorry on board the boat in Plymouth, you have nothing but what can fit inside small knapsacks, which is all the flight organizers have allowed you to bring: a change of clothes and a single favourite item.

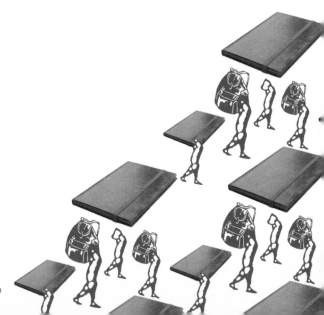

You have brought your diary. It shall remind you that there was a time before the war: a time when Britons were a mixed people allowed to hold differing opinions about everything. A time when you went to Swedish techno parties on Fridays, rode your German roller blades on Saturdays, and ended the weekend with chicken masala at the local Indian food joint. You would holiday at the Fjords of Norway, ski in France, and swim at Spanish beaches. At school you'd pull out your iPhone to see if it was thinner than the Samsungs, Sony-Ericssons and LGs of your friends, while exchanging amicable jokes about the Vikings with your Danish class mate.

It's so endlessly far away that it's like it never was. Even if it was like this only three years ago.

That's what you want to remind yourself of.

That your life has not always been a battle to be all
and totally British, inwardly as well as outwardly. That
Britain has not always been but cold and fear and
mistrust and hatred. That Britain hasn't always had a
Dictator, a Britification Police, and a popular obsession
that to safeguard their freedom and independence, the
British need *preemptively* defend themselves against
barbaric Norse aggression. That the British weren't
always convinced that everything would be better
for the Scandinavians if they would submit to British
overrule in a new British Northern European Empire.
You want to remind yourself that there is another life.
If you forget, then it's as if nothing matters at all. Then
you may just as well enter the Britification Police, or
follow the Militia and your older brother across the
North Sea, shoot Danes until you get shot yourself.

There is another life, and that's what your father will
bring you to now.

Six weeks later you find yourself in Egypt. You live in a tent camp. Hunger no longer gnaws at your guts, there are no missiles or bombs to fear, there is no Britification Police ransacking your home day and night. Your mother has become herself again, and your sister has had the grenade splinters surgically removed. It isn't cold.

Your family's asylum application is being processed, and you can't leave the camp before you're officially recognized as true refugees and will gain temporary permits of residence. It doesn't matter. You are happy. Even if the conditions are terrible, it's only for a while. Half a year at most. Of course you're *true* refugees. What else would you be?

The processing of your application is delayed. Mostly because your brother has become an officer in the Militia. The authorities don't feel convinced about you and your father. You're fourteen, basically a man. And there might be a war raging in your country, but if you could afford to flee you probably weren't that poorly off. Just think of all the people still living in Great Britain. Perhaps they need help more than you do!

Living in the camp wears on you. There is nothing much to do. You aren't taught Arabic because you can only get lessons once you have received the permission to stay. You don't go to school, you aren't allowed to work (and can't anyway, because you don't speak the language). The few books around, you know almost by heart. There is a small recreational square, a gravel ground with a single football goal at one end. It's not its being small that is the issue. As they say, you have to be grateful for having a recreational ground at all. *As if you could play ball amidst the bombs at home.* The issue is that you're so many in the camp, that if everyone shall have their turn, there's hardly any time for each. It's the big guys who play most of the time.

Then, there is something else. Something boiling in you. It's Thorkild and Hans and their crowd in the Danish part of the camp. They keep cursing and worse at you and your new friends. You shall not bring your

animosities into our land, say the Egyptian staff.
So even though the British and Danish refugees in
principle are kept apart, it's only due to the positioning
of the tents. Every time you must fetch water or food,
go to the library or to the recreational square, you have
to pass by the Danish area. These are the people who
destroyed your house, you think every time you pass.
These are the people who killed your grandparents.
That's what you think, even though your father says
that you must never forget that it was the Dictator's
dream of a British Northern European Empire that
started the war. You aren't sure he speaks the truth.
After all, the British had to defend what was theirs.
Remember the Vikings! Who knows what else would
happen. Just look at Thorkild and Hans and their
crowd spitting whenever they see you, shouting '*Fy for
fanden*', hurling pebbles at you. What have you done to
them? As if they are real refugees more than you and
your family!

"Fy For Fanden" "Fy For Fanden" "Fy

أخ   أجنبى   أخ

Fanden" "Fy For Fanden" "Fy For Fa

أخ   أجنبى

"Fy For Fanden" "Fy For Fanden" "F

It's not for lack of heart that you don't strike back. It's only because your father has said again and again that you can't. That if you make the least bit of trouble in the camp, the entire family will immediately be deported back to Britain. So you do nothing. Just feel your blood boil while vowing: one day they'll get what's coming to them!

Two years later you're granted asylum. Temporarily, but that's okay. It took a little extra time because of this matter of your brother and the Militia. Nevertheless, your family belongs to the lucky ones. Many people are sent home. Egypt doesn't have room for more refugees. Housing is short already. Not enough water. Not enough land. You ought to be grateful. Your family has survived, and you can stay here until the war is over. Yet, a rage smoulders within you. It's as if two years of your life were stolen. You haven't finished school, and you have only learned enough Arabic to get by at the market.

Due to a policy about integration and distribution of refugees, your family is obliged to move to Aswan in Southern Egypt. Only one of the families you know from the camp is in Aswan.

Once again, you must start over.

Life is difficult. Everything is different than at home. There are no jobs available, particularly when you are a stranger and don't speak the language. People yell at you in the street, sell you mouldy vegetables at the market and ignore you in the coffee bar. Even though your hair is dark and you get tanned easily, there is no hiding your blue eyes.

After some months, your mother begins to bake biscuits which you and your father sell in the street. Your little sister is cleaning the house for a middle class family that in turn pay her school fees. School is somehow too late for you. You are sixteen. At home you'd have been in high school, here maybe college. But there is no money, so it'll have to wait.

You get used to selling biscuits. You get used to the poverty. And you get used to the extreme heat. You never get used to being looked at as third tier. At home your dad was a lawyer, your mother a professor in history. You had a house in Kensington and two cars. Now you have nothing. You are nothing. Except some unwanted strangers selling biscuits and thereby snatching income possibilities from Egypt's own biscuit sellers.

Every day you swear that one day you'll return to London and resume your life. Your real life. You are going to be a person of first rank once again.

Then you'll show them!

It's only that the war doesn't end. It continues for another year, two, three. Your brother dies in year two. It touches you worryingly little. It's like home is so far away that it doesn't exist.

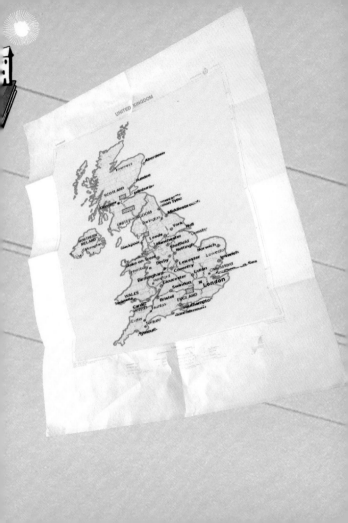

When the war is finally over, Britain is no longer the same country. That's what those say who have been back home. Secretly. If the Egyptian authorities learn that someone has visited Britain, that someone will immediately get expelled. *If you can stay for as long as one day in the country you've fled from, then it must be safe enough for you to remain.* No mention of the ruined houses, the non-existent economy, the peril it is to re-establish oneself formally in a country that has become a dictatorship. Under Danish overrule. Even at home you would be second tier!

In a way it's even worse than during the war. That's what your old classmate Carol writes. People disappear regularly. Before, at least you knew that it was because you weren't British enough. Now no one knows why. People just evaporate. Her older brother is one of them. Shortly after, her father as well. The older brother comes

back, but not the father. Carol's mother wants to get out of the country with her and the brother. But where to?

Egypt doesn't want any more refugees from Northern Europe. Now there's peace, and we can't take any more, they say. Besides, Britons are indecent heathens who corrupt any society that takes them in. The British count themselves superior to everybody, they have no discipline and are unruly and give rise to unrest everywhere, particularly the women, no matter how much you teach them about their host country's ways and habits.

By now you've been in Egypt for five years. You've made friends. Or at least some pals. Mostly other refugees, but also a few Egyptians. You speak Arabic. Like a street boy, but it's sufficient to get by. You also have to translate for your parents, who find it all very complicated.

Your little sister who initially did so well in the all-girl school, got thrown out after eighteen months because she encouraged immoral behaviour and rebellion amongst the girls. She wanted them to learn about sex and contraception. For a short while she was belligerent. Then she fell in love with a thirty-seven year old Egyptian, converted to Islam and began covering her hair and praying five times a day.

Your parents have tried reasoning with her. They are worried about her. She won't listen. What good does their rationale do her here?

She is only sixteen still, and can't decide for herself. They consider sending her home to Britain to live with an aunt for a couple of months. Out of sight, out of mind, as they say. When they do, it's too late. Your sister is pregnant. Your parents nevertheless refuse to let her return to Aswan and marry the child's father. She has to give birth alone in England. She has her entire life ahead of her, they say.

When the child is born, you go home for a week to visit your sister and see if it's time to move back to Britain. It isn't. Among the British who stayed behind during the war, you're considered a traitor. Among the new Danish-leaning authorities, you're listed as an enemy because of your brother's role in the Militia.

To help Carol and her family, you marry Carol. As soon as you get back to Egypt, you apply for family reunion. The rules have been relaxed a little since the stream of refugees from Northern Europe has abated.

It's good to have Carol close by. The sensation of knowing each other from before feels akin to love. Also your parents are happy. You and Carol won't have cultural conflicts, and when one day the situation in Britain improves, you can return together.

The thirty-seven year old Egyptian goes to Britain to convince your sister to marry him. She has turned neo-punk, sniffing something much more exotic than cocaine, wears her hair red and white, has safety pins sticking out of her lower lip, and won't know of him any more. In desperation and concern for the future of his young son, the thirty-seven year old kidnaps the boy and brings him back to Egypt, where he'd been conceived in full anticipation of the parents' matrimony and an upbringing in accordance with Egyptian ways and traditions.

One has to watch out for these Brits. They can't be trusted! As soon as they return home, they change.

You yourself have a child with Carol and ought to be happy. You aren't. Somehow life has turned into something other than it should have been. Someone came and stole your life and turned it into another one. To something neither here nor there.

There's never enough money for you to catch up on your lost education. You no longer feel like studying anyway. Feel embarrassingly aware that you're far behind your contemporaries. You help your father in the bakery that your family has slowly gotten up and running. Carol bakes biscuits together with your mother. You are far from well-off, but you're managing.

You have been granted permanent residency in your new country. Your children are born Egyptians. Their first language is Arabic, and even though they're Christians, they know the Koran better than the Bible. You're on first name terms in the local coffee shop, you are friends with the cobbler and with the car dealer's son, and you're offered the best produce at the market.

Yet, you feel a stranger. Yet, all you think about is when you can go home.

Home where?

AFTERWORD

I originally wrote *If the Nordic Countries were at War* in 2001, when the discussion about refugees in Denmark first seemed to forget that two of our most hailed European philosophical, humanitarian and even Christian, values are: that all human beings are created equal, and to do unto others as you would wish them do unto you. The text was published as a fictional essay in a magazine for Danish teachers. In 2004 a Danish publishing house, Dansklærerforeningens forlag, decided to launch the text as a passport book wonderfully illustrated by Helle Vibeke Jensen.

Coming from a family of Austrian/German refugees and immigrants to Denmark, the thought that life can rapidly be turned upside down by geo-political events has always been very real and tangible for me. But for most Danish Danes, this is not the case. The idea of becoming a refugee is tantamount to the idea of living on Mars. I therefore wrote *War* as an invitation into life as a refugee. Not through the eyes of the refugees come from afar to Denmark. But through their own eyes, their own secure Danish lives turned upside down by a – hopefully – unthinkable war amongst the Nordic countries.

Exactly because this essay was written as an invitation to the imagination, I have always known that in translation it must be adapted to originate in the specific country in question and to its history, culture and geography. Yet, since the essay is in no way intended to rescind or reenact past wars and hostilities, I try to avoid the obvious, and instead make a scenario that is imaginable because it draws upon inner or outer stereotypes, while at the same time evidently being exactly an imagination.

For the United Kingdom, it would have been tempting to build upon the recent Brexit referendum as the catapult for a European war. Yet, no matter my personal passion for the UK to remain part of the European Union, it is not the intent of this book to partake in the immediate political debate, but rather to open roads for understanding and empathy with destinies far from our own. Thus, for Great Britain I chose a nationalistic and autocratic regime, looking to create a British-ruled Northern European Empire in the wake of a European Union that has fallen apart. Claiming the need to pre-empt an attack by the Nordic barbarians, Britain goes to war against Scandinavia. I've thus also taken the opportunity to paraphrase on a Scandinavia that is today no longer the haven of tolerance, humanism, and liberalism, as it is often thought of. Unknowingly, when writing the original, the then far-fledged fiction of a peaceful, democratic and prosperous Middle East has with the Arab spring of 2011 – even if currently marred by the horrors of the Syrian war – perhaps come much closer to reality.

The number of people around the world forced to flee their home countries, due to human and natural disasters, threats to the physical or psychological security of families and individuals, and simple social disparities and lacking economic opportunities, is ever growing. Millions upon millions of normal individual destinies must suddenly see their lives catapulted into refugee-hood. The suffering is in many cases almost incomprehensible. Upon arrival in safer lands, the immediate quest for survival and security in turn becomes about the meeting of cultures, about the capacities and more so the willingness of individuals, as well as groups and nations of people to meet one another. It becomes about the definition of self, both for the ones who *arrive as strangers* as for the ones who *receive the strangers*.

In many ways, I'd have hoped this essay was long obsolete at this point in time. Reality has it, it isn't. Rather on the contrary. Increasingly, when I've been invited to talk about *War* in various countries, I hear it accused of being political. First of all, I've never understood why being political in a political world could be wrong. But secondly, and more importantly, isn't there something awry, something terribly, ominously awry, when the sheer act of trying to envision, to understand and empathize with the situation of *the other* becomes politicized? Aren't we then, already beyond the brink of our own humanity?

I express the hope, therefore, that it isn't the case. I hope understanding is what we, or at least most of us, are still seeking in Europe and across the world. I express the hope that this text will be read un-politically, as the invitation to the imagination that it is. An invitation into the life of *the other*, into what we're all responsible for, shall never become our personal destinies. But if one day it did, wouldn't it be a great comfort to set out on the perilous trails of seeking refuge and better lives elsewhere in the world, with full confidence in the knowledge that when we ourselves had the opportunity to do so, each and every one of us did our share to secure and spread the basic values of human civilization: that all human beings are created equal, and to do unto others as you would wish them do unto you?

Janne Teller,
Guadalajara, 7.3.2013 / Elsinore 19.8.2016

ACKNOWLEDGEMENTS

My particular thanks goes to Jens Raahauge, whom I owe endless gratitude that this text came into existence as a passport book, and to Helle Vibeke Jensen for the amazing illustrations that so poignantly open horizons into the unimaginable.

I owe thanks to numerous people along the way and in many countries for espousing this book – also against much resistance.

For this British version of *War* I owe huge thanks to my publisher Jo Dickinson for her inspiring enthusiasm and support, to Emma Capron for precise and skillful editing, and to my agents Marei Pittner and so very much Charlotte Seymour who found Jo – thus making a match I couldn't wish better – and who has accompanied the text all the way into becoming this book.

I thank my friends and family for bearing with me when, as almost always, I live inside my imagined worlds – for understanding and forgiving the aloofness and guarded solitude that this calls for, and for calling me back ever so often to the realities surrounding me.

I am humbly grateful for all I've learned from the refugees that I worked with or came across, in Tanzania, Mozambique, Uganda and elsewhere – not least in Europe – as to the challenges they face, the horrors they go through, and yet more: the dream that almost everyone harbours of one day being able to go home and resume their lost lives. Lastly, I wish to thank my immigrant family – in particular my Austrian mother and grandmother, as well as my German grandfather – for showing me the difficulties and perilous choices that war forces upon civilians. For making me born into the existence, and thus with the blood-bound understanding of, everything multicultural.

This book is dedicated to all human beings in this world, forced to flee their homes or countries due to war, geo-political conflicts or other reasons beyond their own powers. May they all find safe havens!

Janne Teller is a critically acclaimed and best-selling Danish novelist and essayist of Austrian-German family background.

She has received numerous literary grants and awards, including in 2011 the prestigious American Michael L. Printz Honor Award for Literary Excellency. Her literature, that circles around existential questions of life and civilization and often sparks controversial debate, is today translated into more than 25 languages. Janne Teller has published six novels, including the modern Nordic saga *Odin's Island* about religious and political fanaticism, as well as the existential *Nothing* that after initially being banned, is today considered by many critics a new classic.

Janne Teller is also a human rights activist, and was one of the initiators of the 2013 Writers Against Mass Surveillance campaign. She is a member of the Jury of the prestigious German Peace Prize.